A Canadian YEAR

For Sheryl, world traveller, with love. — TM

For Cody and Raven, forever faithful and always by my side. — TS

A Canadian YEAR

TWELVE MONTHS IN THE LIFE OF CANADA'S KIDS

TANIA MCCARTNEY + TINA SNERLING

Welcome to Canada

Salut! Je m'appelle CHLOE et j'ai 7 ans. We speak both French and English at home. I love art, music and dance, and when I'm older, I want to be a singer.

Ai, I'm OKI. I'm 8 years old and my family are Inuit. We speak Inuktitut. I love travel, languages and science, and I'd love to become a pediatrician one day.

Ni hao! My name is **AVA** and I'm 9. My mom is from China and my dad is from Québec. I love soccer and cooking, and when I grow up, I want to be a chef.

Hey, I'm **LIAM.** My family came to Canada from Scotland. I'm 10, and I love snowboarding and computer games. One day, I want to be a computer programmer.

Hi! My name is **NOAH** and I'm 6 years old. I love reading, football and hiking in the mountains. When I'm big, I want to play hockey for the Vancouver Canucks!

January

It's -30°C but we still go **SKIING**, skating and tobogganing.

BONNE ANNÉE!

It's NEW YEAR'S DAY!

WOOF!

Sled races are **AWESOME**!

There's a lot to keep us **BUSY** after school.

HOCKEY PRACTICE

HOMEWORK

VIDEO GAMES

6 — QUI EST LE ROI?

La FÊTE des Rois.

DOUGHNUTS
AND DOUGHNUT HOLES

COOKIES

CHIPS

FRUIT

CHEESE AND CRACKERS

We have lots of favourite **SNACKS**.

We ride the GONDOLA at Whistler Blackcomb ski resort.

Mom BAKES Nanaimo bars, chocolate chip cookies and butter tarts.

In the north, we ride a SNOWMOBILE to the grocery store!

LUCKY MONEY! AWESOME!

Fireworks welcome CHINESE NEW YEAR.
Kids receive money in red envelopes.

The Québec WINTER CARNIVAL is the largest in the world.

We can play hockey on the Atlantic OCEAN in Newfoundland!

February

On Groundhog Day, Wiarton Willie tells us when SPRING will arrive.

It's a winter WONDERLAND at Winterlude in Ottawa.

We might get a card from a secret admirer on VALENTINE'S DAY.

TEDDY

CANDY

FLOWERS

CARDS

National FLAG of Canada Day

MIAM MIAM!

On Pancake Day, we drizzle our PANCAKES with maple syrup.

It's the Jack Frost Children's WINTERFEST in Charlottetown!

Ananaksaq helps us build an IGLOO in the backyard.

We bake COOKIES and go ice skating on Family Day.

22

It's World THINKING Day.

Montréal en Lumière is pretty DAZZLING!

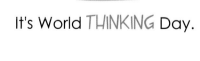

CHINOOKS sweep down from the Rockies and melt our snowmen.

We love our SPORTS.

SOCCER

BASKETBALL

LACROSSE

BASEBALL

DANCE

March

March means SPRING!

Beavers, raccoons and caribou wander the FOREST near our house.

Québec's Hôtel de Glace is made of ICE and SNOW!

SCIENCE IS COOL!

We visit TELUS World of SCIENCE in Edmonton.

The world's largest SKATING RINK, Rideau Canal in Ottawa, starts to thaw.

EPIC!

GREEN BEAR

HORNS

SHAMROCKS

GREEN HATS

17

Montréal's ST PATRICK'S DAY parade is epic!

The skies over our PRAIRIES are so very high.

On GOOD Friday, we nibble hot cross buns, all melty with butter.

It's spring BREAK! Time for Easter, which sometimes falls in April.

CHOCOLATE EGGS

DAFFODILS

CHICKS

BUNNIES

On Easter Sunday, we decorate eggs and go on an EGG HUNT.
We eat mustard-crusted lamb and Easter basket cake.

QUICK! GET IN THE CAR!

DAYLIGHT SAVING begins.
Clocks go forward.

CANADA : 17

Polar BEARS wander the streets of Churchill, Manitoba.

April

1 It's APRIL FOOLS' DAY. We tape paper fish to each other's backs.

POISSON D'AVRIL!

2 It's International Children's BOOK Day!

YELLOW TROUT LILY

BLUE COHOSH

HEPATICAS

WILDFLOWERS start blooming on the forest floor.

Sometimes, EASTER falls in April.

6 National TARTAN Day

SUGAR SHACKS ROCK!

Spring is SWEET at the Sugarbush Maple Syrup Festival.

9

VIMY RIDGE Day

22

On EARTH DAY, we learn how to be green.

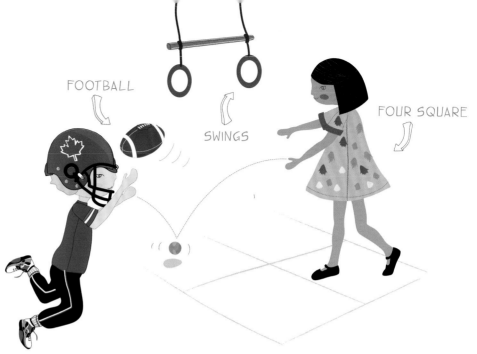

FOOTBALL

SWINGS

FOUR SQUARE

We love to get OUTDOORS during recess and lunch.

SPAGHETTI

SANDWICHES

GRANOLA BAR

FRUIT

We take a LUNCHBOX to school, or eat in the cafeteria.

Mémère and Pépère take us on a trip to NIAGARA FALLS.

May

Our **MOUNTIES** ride beautiful horses.

NEIGH!

FLOWERS
CHOCOLATES

On **MOTHER'S DAY**, we spoil Mom with cards, chocolates and flowers.

We love playing **GAMES** on our TV, iPad and computer.

BURGERS
PASTA
PIZZA
POUTINE
DUMPLINGS
SUSHI
CURRY
PEROGIES

We have **DINNER** around the table.

LOVE TO READ!

It's **BOOK WEEK**! We dive into some stories.

There are a million BLOOMS at the Canadian Tulip Festival!

PRETTY!

VICTORIA Day

It's WARMING up. We ride our bikes, go skateboarding or play soccer in the park.

We celebrate our CULTURE with powwows and potlatches.

We like CANDY!

Yogi Bear lives at JELLYSTONE Park.

It's the Ottawa CHILDREN'S Festival.

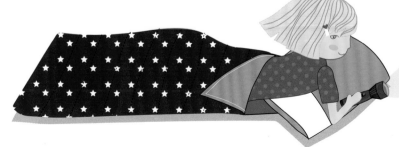

We have sleepovers and playdates with FRIENDS.

June

It's SUMMER. More than two months off school!

YÉ!

Some of us go to summer CAMPS.

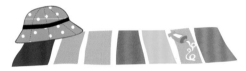

We spoil our dad on FATHER'S DAY.

WORLD'S BEST DAD

KARATE

KAYAKING

ROCK CLIMBING

Everyone heads to the local SWIMMING pool.

RAMADAN can fall in different months of the year.

Canada's WONDERLAND is awesome!

Winnipeg International CHILDREN'S Festival

21

On National Aboriginal Day, we celebrate our **INDIGENOUS** people with festivals and feasts.

SANTA has a summer home just outside Toronto!

SANTA'S VILLAGE FAMILY ENTERTAINMENT PARK

It's the Toronto **PRIDE** Parade!

27

BONJOUR! HELLO! AI! NI HAO!

On Canadian **MULTICULTURALISM** Day, we celebrate the many cultures that make our country great.

Dad takes us **SALMON** fishing in the Pacific Ocean!

BLACK BEAR   CARIBOU

BEAVER   RACCOON

Our **CAMPING** trips take us deep into the wilderness.

Celebration of Light in Vancouver is a spectacular musical FIREWORKS competition.

WOW!

ORCAS can be spotted off the coast of Vancouver.

LEMONADE   JUICE   MILK   WATER

We COOL down with our favourite drinks.

Our family has a weiner roast on the BEACH.

Granville Island Water Park is SPLASHING good fun.

August

Piikani Nation Annual Celebration is Canada's oldest POWWOW event.

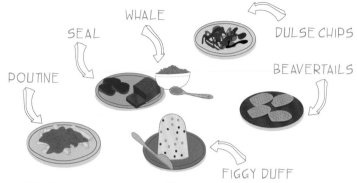

SEAL
WHALE
DULSE CHIPS
POUTINE
BEAVERTAILS
FIGGY DUFF

We have some pretty QUIRKY Canadian foods.

FREEZIES cool us down.

National PEACEKEEPERS' Day

AH, THE GREAT OUTDOORS!

Our allowance is paid in LOONIES and TOONIES.

Papa takes us camping on LAKE SUPERIOR. We hunt, fish and swim.

September

ALSO CALLED AUTUMN

It's FALL. Leaves start to turn.

The SCHOOL YEAR begins.

On LABOUR DAY, we go to a local fair, have a picnic or watch football on TV.

FÊTE DU TRAVAIL

EGGS   BANNOCK   WAFFLES

HONEY

MILK

CEREAL   SMOOTHIE   PANCAKES

BREAKFAST is scrumptious at our house.

We tell tales at the Telling Tales children's LITERARY FESTIVAL in Rockton, Ontario.

Local MOOSE, bears and raccoons knock over our garbage can!

We go on a field trip to the **MARITIME** Museum of the Atlantic in Halifax.

National **GRANDPARENTS'** Day

LEGO

BOARD GAMES

LEGO

DOLLS

On **RAINY** days, we play inside.

The Canadian Aboriginal Festival celebrates our **FIRST NATIONS** people.

PUMPKIN

APPLES

CORN

MAPLE SYRUP

OOOH!

The **NORTHERN LIGHTS** are a sight to behold.

Local **FESTIVALS** are held around Canada all through the year.

October

5

KATSURA

SUGAR MAPLE

AMERICAN BEECH

RED OAK

BLACK TUPELO

You can adopt an **ANIMAL** at Toronto Zoo.

National **FAMILY** Week

Our fall **LEAVES** are mesmerizing.

OGOPOGO has been seen in Lake Okanagan!

BUGS! NEAT!

INSECTS

Aanak shows us how to make **BANNOCK**.

FLOUR

The Montréal Insectarium is **CREEPY** and cool.

On THANKSGIVING, we feast with family and friends. Some of us go hiking or fishing.

SECOND MONDAY IN OCTOBER

Migrating BIRDS fly high in the skies above.

WHOOPING CRANE

GOLDEN EAGLE

CANADA GOOSE

TUNDRA GOOSE

There are farm animals, corn mazes and hayrides at our local PUMPKIN PATCH.

Dad loves OKTOBERFEST!

BOO!

R.I.P.

31

It's HALLOWEEN! We trick-or-treat, carve pumpkins, and gobble toffee apples and candy.

DAYLIGHT SAVING ends.

Clocks go back.

POUR QU'ON SE SOUVIENNE

Lest We Forget

11

The Last Post rings out on REMEMBRANCE Day. Lest We Forget.

We catch the bus, ride a bike or walk to SCHOOL.

RINK RAT

TOQUE

BUNNYHUG

SCARF

GLOVES

SNOW PANTS

We gear up for WINTER.

SKATES

The male CARIBOU sheds his antlers at this time of year.

HAPPY NEW YEAR!

Diwali Festival of LIGHTS rings in the Hindu New Year.

In Banff National Park, the WILDLIFE have overpasses!

Grandma shows us how to weave DREAM CATCHERS.

20

It's Universal CHILDREN'S Day.

The WINTER FESTIVAL of Lights in Niagara Falls begins.

'INUIT' means 'the people'. Our anoraks are made from caribou hide and sealskin.

In Northern Canada, our HOMES are built on stilts so the ground below doesn't melt!

December

WINTER is here. It's all snowball fights and snow forts.

Our Christmas tree smells like the FOREST.

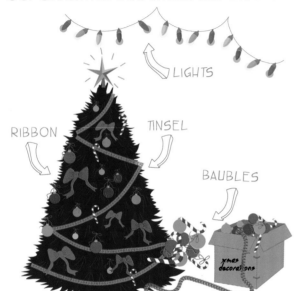

LIGHTS

RIBBON

TINSEL

BAUBLES

xmas decorations

We make gingerbread and write in CHRISTMAS cards.

CALGARY ROUGHNECKS!

TORONTO ROCK!

The National LACROSSE League season begins.

10 It's HUMAN RIGHTS DAY.

The Santa Claus parade in Toronto is MASSIVE!

HANUKKAH

We eat maple syrup TAFFY, barley candy and chicken bones!

JE M'APPELLE PÈRE NOËL

French families enjoy RÉVEILLON on Christmas Eve.
We dine on tourtières and bûche de Noël.

24

On Christmas Eve, we track Santa's journey online.
Some of us open PRESENTS or go to Midnight Mass.

It's Christmas HOLIDAYS!

ROAST TURKEY

HAM

GRAVY

SINCK TUCK is celebrated
with dancing and gift-giving.

CRANBERRY SAUCE

PEAS

MASHED POTATO

PLUM PUDDING

APPLE PIE

25

On CHRISTMAS DAY, we open
presents and enjoy a delicious feast.

It's BOXING Day. 26

BONNE ANNÉE!

31

We go ice-fishing on NEW YEAR'S EVE.
Fireworks pop to welcome in a brand new year.

Our Country

THE PROVINCES AND TERRITORIES OF CANADA

Alberta
British Columbia
Manitoba
New Brunswick
Newfoundland and Labrador
Nova Scotia
Ontario
Prince Edward Island
Québec
Saskatchewan
Northwest Territories
Nunavut
Yukon

CANADA IS THE WORLD'S SECOND-LARGEST COUNTRY

THE NORTH AMERICAN BEAVER IS OUR NATIONAL ANIMAL

CANADA HAS THE LONGEST COASTLINE IN THE WORLD

AFTER PARIS, MONTRÉAL IS THE LARGEST FRENCH-SPEAKING CITY IN THE WORLD

Canada comes from the native word 'kanata' meaning village.

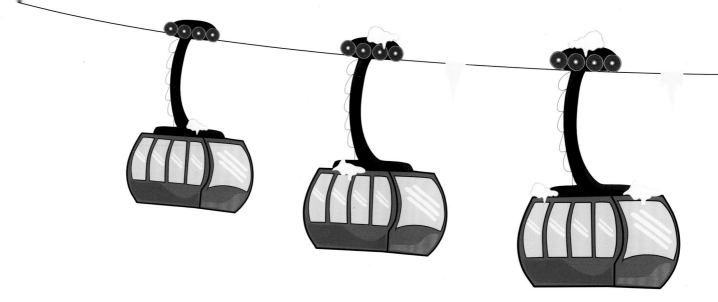

A huge thank you to Canadian advisors Kathy Bobyn, Helen Busetti, and to the kids of Ripple Rock Elementary, British Columbia. Thanks also to the following people for their contribution: Ellen Warwick, Iolanda Millar, Jacques Filippi, Jean Cichon, Kristina Koski, Peter Hill-Field, Tim Gain and Tracey Bhangu. Unending thanks to Anouska Jones and the team at Exisle for their support.
— TM + TS

This Little Passports edition published 2020
First published 2017

EK Books
An imprint of Exisle Publishing Pty Ltd
P.O. Box 864, Chatswood, NSW 2057, Australia
226 High Street, Dunedin 9016, New Zealand
www.ekbooks.org

A CiP record for this book is available from the National Library of Australia

ISBN 978 1 925820 54 6

Designed and typeset by Tina Snerling
Typeset in Century Gothic, Street Cred and custom fonts

Printed in China

This book uses paper sourced under ISO 1 4001 guidelines from well-managed forests and other controlled sources.

10 9 8 7 6 5 4 3 2

Author Note

This is by no means a comprehensive listing of the events and traditions celebrated by Canada's multitude of ethnic people. The entries in this book have been chosen to reflect a range of modern lifestyles for the majority of Canada's children, with a focus on traditional endemic elements and themes, which are in themselves a glorious mishmash of present, past, introduced and endemic culture. Content in this book has been produced in consultation with native Canadian advisors, school teachers, and school children, with every intention of respecting the cultural and idiosyncratic elements of Canada and its people.